The Magical Tree-Castle

First published in Great Britain 1995 by Heinemann Young Books
an imprint of Egmont Children's Books Limited
Michelin House, 81 Fulham Rd, London SW3 6RB.
Mammoth paperback edition first published 1998.
Published in hardback by Heinemann Library,
a division of Reed Educational and Professional Publishing Limited
by arrangement with Egmont Children's Books Limited.
Text copyright © Douglas Hill 1995
Illustrations copyright © Ben Cort 1995
Additional illustrations copyright © Ben Cort 1998
The Author and Illustrator have asserted their moral rights.
Paperback ISBN 0 7497 3558 9
Hardback ISBN 0 434 80400 2
10 9 8 7 6 5 4 3 2
A CIP catalogue record for this title is available from the British Library
Printed at Oriental Press Limited, Dubai

Douglas Hill

The Magical Tree-Castle

Illustrated by BEN CORT

 YELLOW BANANAS

For Sean D.
happy climbing

Chapter One

Leafy Arm

WHEN DORA'S FATHER asked her what she wanted for her birthday, she didn't have to stop and think.

'A tree-house!' she said.

She knew exactly which tree she wanted it in too – the giant old oak tree that stood at the bottom of the garden.

To Dora the oak seemed a hundred feet high. Its long, thick branches stretched up and up, with smaller branches and leaves spraying in all directions. But there was one huge lower branch that bent downwards in a swooping curve, as if the tree was reaching down with a long leafy arm.

It was one of Dora's favourite places. She never grew tired of sitting on the big low branch, listening to the birds, or being thrilled by the fearless games of the squirrels. And then, there was also the owl.

Dora almost never saw the owl. But often, in the late afternoon or early evening, she would hear its cry from the oak tree. The cry began with a shivery 'hoooooo!' and then became a high, sharp call sounding like 'wheet!' or 'whit!' Sometimes it even sounded like 'twit!' as if the owl was scolding someone, which made Dora smile.

So, because she loved the tree and its creatures, she had the idea of having a tree-house for her birthday.

'All right,' Dora's father said. 'I could make a play-house for you on that big low branch where you're always sitting.'

'That would be lovely,' Dora said.

So her father set to work.

And because he was good at making things, it turned out to be an amazing house. It had a floor of wooden boards nailed on to the big branch, and brightly painted wooden walls, and a clear plastic sheet for a roof so Dora could see up into the tree. And there were big openings like windows on every side, so she could see all around the garden.

Best of all, just for fun, her father had shaped the sides so that each corner rose up above the roof.

'Oh!' Dora gasped, when she saw it. 'It's like a castle!'

'That's it,' her father said, smiling. 'Not a tree-house but a tree-castle. For a princess on her birthday.'

Thanking him with a hug, Dora scrambled up into the tree-castle. She thought it was the most perfect birthday present ever as she gazed up at the birds and the leafy shadows.

It wasn't until the next day that she found out the tree-castle was magical.

Chapter Two
Bird Words

AS SOON AS she could, the next day, Dora
moved properly into her tree-castle. She took
a sandwich and a drink with her, two books
and some paper and coloured pens so she
could draw the tree and its creatures.

But when she was settled, feeling cosy and
private and delighted, she never got around to

drawing or reading. It was much more fun just to sit and enjoy the show around her in the tree – a squabble among sparrows, an acrobatic game of chase-me by the squirrels, a burst of song from a blackbird.

Yet Dora began to notice, as the day went on, that none of the little creatures came anywhere near her. They're afraid of the tree-castle, she thought. So she scattered some crumbs on to the branch outside, to show the birds that she was a friend.

A brave little sparrow was the first to come. Watching her carefully, it pecked at a few crumbs, then put its head on one side and chirped.

To Dora's astonishment, the chirp sounded just like words.

The sparrow had said 'thank you'.

'You're welcome,' Dora said blankly, before she could stop herself.

The sparrow nearly fell off the branch. Then it rocketed away, up into the tree, shrilling with alarm.

'She talked! *Talked!*' the sparrow was calling. '*Spoke* to me!'

Dora drew back from the tree-castle window, wide-eyed with shock. She could talk with the birds! She could understand what every one of them was saying, and they could understand her as well.

A moment later, a big blackbird swooped down and peered into the tree-castle at Dora.

'Did you speak?' it chirruped. 'Did you? Speak to me! If you can! Can you?'

Dora opened her mouth, but no sound came from her throat.

The blackbird flicked its tail. 'See?' it called.

'Can't speak! People can't! Not to birds! Silly idea! Crazy sparrow idea!'

That seemed unfair to Dora, as well as untrue. And it unlocked her voice.

'The sparrow *isn't* crazy!' she said loudly.

The entire tree went utterly silent. Then the squirrels peered nervously around the tree-trunk.

'Can she talk . . .' one squirrel began.

' . . . to us too?' added the other squirrel.

Dora struggled to find her voice again. 'Yes,' she said. 'I can.'

A sharp-eyed starling hopped down to a lower branch and looked in the window.

'How can you?' it squawked. 'People can't! Why can you?'

'I don't know,' Dora said. 'It just happened.' She looked around at them. 'You mustn't be afraid. I'm not going to hurt you. I'd never hurt a bird.'

'That's so,' said a wood pigeon. 'She just sits. Never climbs. Never throws a stone. Never anything. Just sits.'

'It's all I want to do,' Dora said. 'Just sit here. I won't even talk to you if it scares you.'

'No. You must talk,' the blackbird said. 'We will all talk together. It will be fun.'

Then, from near the top of the giant oak, another bird raised its voice – sounding sleepy and puzzled and a bit cross.

'Hooooo!' the owl said. 'What?'

Chapter Three
Just Owl

AS THE BIRDS and squirrels fled in all directions, the owl floated down towards Dora. It was smaller than Dora expected, but it was still a bit scary, with its claws and hooked beak.

Dora drew back a little. 'You wouldn't hurt me, would you?'

'Who?' the owl said, sounding offended. 'Twit!'

Dora giggled nervously at being called a twit by a bird. 'I'm sorry I woke you up.'

'So am I,' the owl said. 'But I see now what all the fuss was about. A human talking to birds!'

'I wish I knew how it happened,' Dora said.

'Magic,' the owl told her. 'There are always bits of magic floating

around these very
old trees. That's
why folk like elves
lived in old forests.
And when this thing
was built . . .'

'Tree-castle,'
corrected Dora.

'As you say,' the owl went on. 'Anyway, it's
just in the right place – and somehow just the
right size and shape and colour and
everything – to gather up the tree's magic. So
now you can speak to us. As long as you're
inside it.'

'That's wonderful,' Dora said, delighted to
find that owls really were quite wise, just as
they were supposed to be. Then she
remembered to be polite. 'Oh, my name's
Dora. What's yours?'

'Just call me Owl,' the owl said, blinking.
'Birds don't have names.' And he spread his
wings and flew back to the top of the tree.

Chapter Four
Tree Magic

THAT SUMMER, DORA spent most of every day in her tree-castle. Each day she took crumbs for the birds and nuts for the squirrels, and each day her new friends gathered around her. They pecked at the crumbs and nibbled at the nuts, but most of all they talked and talked happily, on and on.

Before long, Dora found that the magic of the tree-castle could reach out beyond the

tree. She and Owl had been watching her
father trying to get rid of the greenfly on his
flowers. And Owl calmly told her that she
could simply tell the pests to go away.

So, after her father had gone in, and although she felt a bit foolish, Dora tried it. 'All you greenfly,' she called. 'Get out of this garden!'

Amazingly, in a huge cloud, the greenfly rose from her father's plants and flew away.

So Dora used the magic to drive away the caterpillars and beetles and slugs that were also eating the plants, while useful insects like bees and ladybirds were invited in.

Another day, Dora heard a burst of
frightened twittering from the birds. From her
tree-castle, she saw a big ginger cat on the
garden fence.

Again, Dora tried the magic. 'You! Cat!' she
shouted. 'Stop scaring my friends!'

The cat froze on the fence,
its fur standing on end.

'You *spoke* to me!' hissed the terrified cat.

'Go away!' Dora yelled. 'And tell the other cats to stay away too!'

With a yowl, the cat vanished from the fence. And from then on, not one of the neighbourhood cats ever prowled through Dora's garden.

So the summer went on, with Dora having the happiest time of her life in her tree-castle with her friends.

Until happiness ended – in the face of a more fearful danger than Dora could have imagined.

Chapter Five
Monster Wind

IT BEGAN ONE evening, when her father heard on the news that a huge and powerful wind – almost a hurricane – was blowing out at sea. And it was feared that the wind might move inland and head towards the town where Dora lived.

'It had better not,' her father said. And he told Dora how such a terrible wind could damage roofs, blow cars off roads and rip trees up by the roots.

'Trees?' Dora said fearfully. 'Would it hurt our old tree?'

'It could,' her father said. 'A tree that size, as old as that . . .'

'I hope it won't fall on the house,' her mother said.

With those grim thoughts in mind, Dora slipped out to the tree-castle. She wanted to collect her books and pens in case the storm came. But mostly she wanted to warn Owl about the danger.

As soon as she was in the tree-castle, Owl floated silently down through the deepening shadows of dusk.

'Hoo,' he said worriedly, when Dora had told him about the storm that might come their way. 'A monster wind. That could be very bad.'

'Will you be all right?' Dora asked. 'And the other birds?'

'Oh, yes,' Owl said. 'Birds know how to get through a big wind. It's the tree I'm worried about. It's very old and perhaps not as strong as it once was.'

'That's what my Dad thought,' Dora said unhappily.

Owl peered at her. 'Could you stay here, Dora? To help the tree if the wind comes?'

'Stay? In the tree-castle?' Dora was startled. 'Oh, I couldn't, Owl. I'm sorry. I'd never be allowed out after dark.'

'Hoooo,' the owl said again. 'I thought not. Never mind. Maybe the wind won't come after all.'

And he spread his wings and drifted away as Dora went back into the house.

Dora spent the rest of the evening worrying.
And later, after she had finally got to sleep,
she was awakened in the middle of the night
by some frightening noises. Her window was
rattling and crashing as if it were about to
break. And outside, even louder, she heard a
raging howl. A wild gale-force wind that was
shaking the whole house with its fury.

Dora got up and crept to the window. She gasped as she looked out at the garden. Even in the darkness, she could see flowers and other low plants being flattened by the wind. And smaller trees and bushes were bent almost double, with many broken branches. Even the mighty oak tree was bending, its branches whipping in the wind. And the thin walls of the tree-castle were jerking and flapping under the gale's monstrous power.

Dora went cold with fear. Not just for her tree-castle, but for the oak tree itself and all its little creatures. And for her parents' house, if the tree fell. 'But it mustn't fall,' she said to herself. 'It mustn't!'

She leaned closer to the window, wishing there was something she could do. Then she had the weirdest feeling . . . as if she was floating, as if she was drifting into the air . . .

And all at once she was there, in the darkened tree-castle, in her nightgown.

Chapter Six
Invisible Shield

THE HOWLING WIND had turned the oak tree into a thrashing frenzy. Even the huge, low branch that held the tree-castle was heaving and bucking like a wild horse. Desperately, Dora clung to the edge of one window and was astounded to see Owl clinging to the opposite window.

Owl clawed his way across to her. 'Don't be afraid, Dora!' he said. 'You'll be safe here in your castle.'

'But how did I get here?' Dora wailed. 'What's happening?'

'I don't think you're really here,' Owl said. 'You're having a dream. And because you were so worried about the tree, and us, your dreaming self has come out. Maybe the magic in your castle helped to bring you. So why don't you *use* the magic, Dora, to fight the wind?'

The tree-castle lurched again as the branch beneath it heaved, and Dora heard the oak tree give a 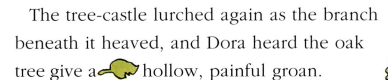 hollow, painful groan.

'Stop it!' she shouted at the gale. 'You're not going to smash my tree-castle! You're not, you're *not!*'

In the next instant, amazingly, she had the feeling that the wind had changed. It was swerving around the tree-castle so that where Dora sat it was perfectly calm. But the gale was still battering at the old oak. Dora heard another groan from the tree as slowly it began to be uprooted.

'Dora!' Owl cried. 'Use the magic for the

tree! Please, Dora! Save the tree!'

'Leave the tree alone!' Dora yelled at the gale. 'Stop pulling it up! Leave it alone!'

The gale screamed even more wildly, but as before, the wind seemed to swerve around the tree. Suddenly the old oak stopped groaning and the branches and leaves stopped thrashing.

But by using the magic to save the tree, Dora had taken it away from the tree-castle. And at once, as if in revenge, the wind hurled a furious gust.

The tree-castle's plastic roof tore like tissue paper. The walls split apart as the wind struck them. And Dora, inside, screamed in panic as she felt the full force of that terrible gust.

'No!' she screamed. 'Stop . . .'

But the voice of Owl was also a scream, sharp and frantic. 'Don't, Dora! If you use the magic to save your tree-castle, the tree will fall! You must let the castle go to save the tree!'

Dora hesitated, desperately unwilling to lose her tree-castle. And in that moment of hesitation, the wind had its way. The walls of the tree-castle ripped apart. Snapping and splintering, the boards whirled away into the darkness.

Dora felt herself fly into the air as the tree-castle was destroyed around her. She fell back with a thump on to the big low branch, where only one floor-board still remained, hanging from two stout nails. Frantically she grabbed for it, missed, felt herself rolling
off the branch,
felt herself falling . . .

Chapter Seven
Nothing Left

DORA WOKE UP in her bed, with the early
morning light streaming through her curtains.
She sat up, startled. Had the magic really
saved the tree or was it just an ordinary
dream? Jumping out of bed, she ran to the
window to see.

The garden was covered in branches and
leaves. Most of the low plants were ruined,
the small trees bent and broken. And there

was nothing at all left of her tree-castle –
except one broken floor-board, hanging by
two nails from the big low branch.

But the giant oak tree still stood, tall and
splendid, spreading its branches to the
morning sun.

So it happened, Dora thought. I was out
there in my dream, and the magic did save the
tree.

Dressing quickly,
she went downstairs
to find her parents
making breakfast and
talking about the gale
and the near-disaster.

'That's a strong old
tree,' her father was saying. 'You can see
where the roots started coming up – but
somehow it held on.'

'Just as well for our house,' her mother said.

'Too bad about your tree-house, though,
Dora,' her father said. 'Would you like me to
build you another?'

Dora sighed, remembering what Owl had
said.

Her tree-castle had been made exactly the
right way – by pure luck – to gather up the
old tree's magic. But a new tree-castle could
never be magical, because it could never be
exactly like the first one.

'No,' she said at last. 'I don't think I want
another, thank you.'

She wandered out to the oak tree. All the
birds and squirrels were still there, unharmed.
But the sounds they made were only
twitterings and chatterings.

'Oh,' said Dora sadly. 'It's gone. We can't
talk any more.'

Then a voice said 'Whoooo?' and the owl
swooped down, peering from a lower branch.

'Owl,' Dora said hopefully. 'Can you still
talk to me?'

Slowly the owl turned his head from one
side to the other, as if saying 'no'.

Dora blinked back tears. Then she
looked up at the beautiful old oak
tree. The birds were singing
peacefully and the squirrels
were playing chase-me up
and down the trunk.

'I had to save the tree, didn't I?' Dora said at last. 'I suppose it was worth it . . .'

The owl blinked at her, solemnly, silently.

'And you won't stop being my friend, will you, Owl?' Dora pleaded.

'Who?' the owl said clearly. 'Twit!'

And he closed one yellow eye in a large cheerful wink.

More Yellow Bananas
by *Douglas Hill* !

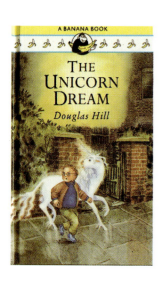

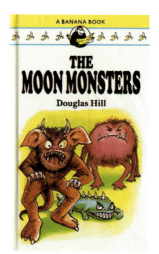

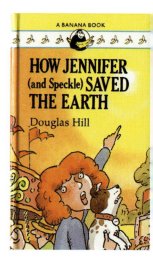

Yellow Bananas are bright, funny, brilliantly imaginative stories written by some of today's top writers. All the books are beautifully illustrated in full colour.

So if you've enjoyed this story, why not pick another one from the bunch?

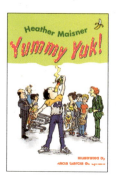

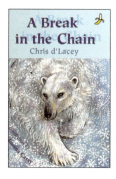

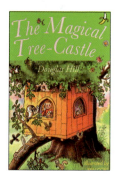